King of the Toast
Joe Zux

A collection of 75 poems

Copyright Joe Landers 2023
All rights reserved. No portion of this book may be reproduced in any form without written permission from the author, except as permitted by U.K. copyright law.

For Aspen, Ellie and Wren

My second book. This contains more of my poetry and ramblings from Love to Political, with a whole gamut of subjects covered in-between. With a different subject of matters including farts and burning toast, which lent its name to the book and poem of the same name.

Massive thank you to all those who support me, I hope you enjoy this new collection as much as I enjoyed writing them.

I have a bandcamp page where you can find audio versions of some of my work joezux.bandcamp.com

I also have a Facebook group called:
Joe Zux : Poetry 'N' Stuff, feel free to join.

Contents

Heads Up - 5
Does It End - 6
Looking Glass - 7
Sat In a Cafe - 8
Dot And Dash - 10
Electronica - 11
Heart And Feel - 12
Scream - 13
I'm Still Someone - 14
Dark Dog Come Again - 15
Knuckle Draggers and Flag Shaggers - 16
Trying Political - 17
Me And You - 19
Haunt Their Dream - 20
Missiles Of Your Mind - 21
Collar - 22
Neuro Divergent Head - 23
Still Sing Protest Songs - 25
Stood in My Garden - 27
King of the Toast - 28
Not The Same - 29
Mark Wants a Banjo - 30
Gammon Bloke - 31
The People Should Start Revolting - 32
Controlled TV - 34
White Soap Powder - 35
I Believe - 38
Hello - 40
See Myself for Real - 41
Prime Control - 43
Your Eyes - 44
A Simple Love Piece - 45
My Twee Weepy Left Tit - 46
12-12-22 - 47
Please Be Direct - 49
For James - 50
The Void - 51
The Beginning - 52
The Dog Joke One - 53
Two Words Two Views - 54

They Shall Not Pass - 55
Exit The Cage - 56
Puppet - 57
Lest We Forget - 60
Stay Grounded - 61
Reflected Reality - 63
Self-Entitled - 64
Frozen Raspberries and Pineapple - 65
Bubbles - 65
Shut The Fuck Up - 66
Farts Innit - 67
Nameless Face - 68
Boris Fucked My Barbecue - 69
5 & 6 - 70
For Mark - 71
Dishy Rishi - 72
As You Have Gone - 73
Larry Cat PM - 74
See You - 75
Sweat - 75
Where You Came From - 76
Bad Addiction - 77
Where Did the Words Go - 77
Make Your Bed in the Morning - 78
Privileged Piss - 78
Alone - 79
Your World - 81
Ginger Cat - 82
About Time - 83
You're Not an Anchor - 84
Her Words, My Music, Our Song - 85
Inner Chimp and Anxiety versus Relationships - 86
Hello you - 88
To Gain - 89
Bookmarks - 90

Heads Up

So I'm on the tube train,
And we're totally stuck again,
Ridiculously running late now,
It's starting to driving me insane.

I have lots of places I have to be,
A multitude of things I need to do,
Can't believe we're not moving yet,
Seems I've been stuck an hour or two.

Everybody jostling each other,
Trying to find a bit of room,
Packed tightly in like sardines,
It's hot and I may start to swoon.

Comment over the announcement system,
Tube drivers' words makes me guffaw,
A commuter who is running late,
Got his head stuck in the door.

It's the way calm way he said it,
Announced it as a statement of fact,
"Well, well, well, ladies and gentlemen,
We seem to have caught ourselves a twat".

Does It End

Memories of imagination,
Or just a figment in my mind,
Captured pictures from the past,
Flickering through my mind,
Lost in a timeless capsule,
Trying to break through.

Walking on the cliff edge,
Hoping the path doesn't crumble down,
Fighting the urge to jump of the precipice,
Fall into the crashing waves of memories,
Open my mouth, suffocate and drown.

Washed up on an island of dreams,
Good times and bad times are the scene,
One door opens to the future,
The other to the past so it seems,
Filling my lungs with bitterness to scream.

Life's evolving circle,
Incessantly drumming in my head,
Oblivious of steps going forever forwards,
One day is it now or before,
So it continues until I'm dead.

Looking Glass

We can peer through the looking glass,
See a reflection of what might've been,
Is it reality or truth,
Or just a caterpillar's dream.

Looking at past actions,
With a different path they took,
Are you scared of what might have been?
Brave enough to take that look.

What if you chose the wrong bottle?
Realise you didn't want this life that grew,
Is it too late to change your direction?
Should it have been the red pill not blue.

Is it too late to change it?
Start your story book anew,
Are you trapped in this situation?
Which side of the looking glass are you?

Sat In a Cafe

Could have fallen for racism,
Bought up in a town that was white,
Institutional blinkers,
The propaganda of the 70's before my eyes.
Bernard Manning on television,
Even Jim Davidson too,
Then the local " ooh we don't want them here",
I could have swallowed it all as true.

Love thy neighbour on television,
Mind your language with its stereotypes,
All there to mould a young mind,
Hearing all that NF rhetoric tripe.

What opened my eyes,
To break this stupid scene,
Sitting in a cafe at seven,
Still vividly remember the scene.
A Sikh family walking in to the local cafe,
A young lad with his hair tied up and covered,
Members of my family,
Innocently thinking they're having a laugh,
"Look at him with a jam pot cover on his head".

So I looked,
All I saw was an embarrassed teenager,
Looking at the floor over and over again,
Then I looked at my family members,
Never felt so much embarrassment or ashamed.
I could have ignored it,
Not said a solitary word,
But I said I see a kid just like me,
Because that was all I observed.

Then I started questioning everything,
Start looking at the white,
Didn't take me long to realise,
They were living in fright.

Swallowing all the bullshit,
Looking for people to blame,
Devouring the propaganda,
Like the 1930's all over again.

So each day is a journey,
Listening to people tell tales of hate,
Do I understand what it's like to be abused racially?
No,
But I will always open my gate.

Dot and Dash

It all started so innocently just a dash and a dot,
The message a portent, 'What hath god wrought',
The clue was there at the very start,
Fallen into a world where everyone knows everything thing,
This age of information, out of control cannot be caught.

Cables laid across the ocean,
Linking what should never have been,
From Ireland's Valentia Island to America's Trinity Bay,
Bringing news from afar at first a dream.

Technology never stops forever gaining momentum,
The key finally opening Pandora's box,
The truth forgotten in distant memory,
Don't fit the narrative it's quickly dropped.

A world of lies and misinformation,
Guiding us blindly down this path,
Leading us into hate and temptation,
Devil rosin his fiddle ready, having a laugh.

It's far too late now to halt it,
The world now carried in our pocket,
Hypnotised by flickering dreams and screens,
Human race addicted like a drug,
Far too late now to begin to stop it.

To think it all started off so innocently,
The world connected with a code made of a dot and a dash,
Until the world eventually starts burning,
No more joy, fun or anyone left to laugh.

All destroyed by on creeping technology,
The genie is let out the warped twisted bottle,
With his hands tightly round humanity's neck,
The path is too late to reverse,
As slowly he starts to throttle.

Electronica

Electronica Robots doing a square dance,
Circuitry buzzing see them prance.

Binary noise sounding loud,
Synthesised dreams they're all proud.

From the smallest electronic till,
All with unique sounds making you chill.

Myriad of noise, senses abound,
Mixed to make a melodic sound.

Fragments of noise you thought you once knew,
Captured lost lyrics in the moment of true.

Electronic melody creeping within,
Powered together in electrical sin.

Heart and Feel

See the stars shining bright above,
Floating in the night sky, powered by love.
Dreams are reality anything is real,
All you have to do is open your heart and feel.

Grasp the moment it could be our last,
Euphoric memories fading into the past.
Sounds rhythmic flowing through your veins,
Like synapse firing, powering your brain.

Speeding each moment none the same,
Life speeding past stuck in the fast lane.
Grab it, hold it, keep it oh so tight,
Adrenaline pumping ready to fight.

See the stars shining bright above,
Floating in the night sky, powered by love.
All together fists raised high to the sky,
Shouting from our lungs this is our battle cry.

Sweating pulsating lost in the beat,
Energy flowing generating heat.
Never deny or give in on the day,
Everything we believe in comes our way.

Want it, got it, this is all mine,
Chant it, shout it, life is fine.
Wanting, holding, love is enough,
Soaring high like a white winged dove.

See the stars shining bright above,
Floating in the night sky, powered by love.

Scream

With my feet on the ground,
And my head in the clouds,
Lost in my inner space,
Closed to all sounds,
Not knowing what is real,
Not aware of what I feel,
No longer sure of myself,
Am I real or a toy on a shelf,
Do I come out of a box to play?
I'm just a looping program,
Not even aware of the day,
The people I see,
Are they actually here,
Am I lost in memories,
Is this not reality I fear,
Just watching hands turn,
All on my invisible clock,
Thoughts are just fractions,
Will this ever stop,
Am I awake or just asleep,
Lost in my life like it's a dream,
Like that famous Munch painting,
All I want to do is scream.

I'm Still Someone

The race is over and run,
I'm still someone.
The race is over and run,
I'm still someone.

Take another drink,
Drown your sorrows away,
Put another coin in the slot,
Make it go away.

Looking for oblivion,
In the bottom of the glass,
Mixed up memories,
Of a broken past,

The race is over and run,
I'm still someone.
The race is over and run,
I'm still someone.

Worn so many hats,
Don't know which is me,
Looking for a way out,
Trying to be free.

Smoke filled stares,
Yeah, all directed at me,
Looking for the answers,
Lost in smoky burgundy.

So top the glass back up,
Leave the bottle by my side,
Trying to get out of this past,
I may just be here a while.

The race is over and run,
I'm still someone.
The race is over and run,
I'm still someone.

The race is over and run,
I'm still someone.
The race is over and run,
I'm still someone.

Dark Dog Come Again

Dark dog come again,
Brought his whole pack,
Trying to bring loathing and blame,
Going to dig deep and send him back.

No food for you here,
No feeding on my emotions,
Hope my message is very clear,
Going to dig deep and use my potions.

Turn on my music for a happy feel,
Use the sound to enter a trance,
The sounds of happiness to make it real,
Singing along and doing an outrageous dance.

Knuckle Draggers and Flag Shaggers

Ever see a small boat cross the sea,
Trying to make the other side?
Ever seen a young girl living in terror'
Trying to make herself a life?
So life becomes better, my love?
When we have finally got rid of,
Knuckle Draggers and Flag Shaggers,
That your poor old granddad,
Had to fight in '36 to deny them.

Once I was a young man,
And all I thought I had to do is protest,
Well, you are still a young girl,
And you're shouting against this vitriolic bile,
So once you agree with this, you're out ',
Cause life will be a better thing without,
Knuckle Draggers and Flag Shaggers,
That your poor old granddad,
Had to fight in '36 to deny them.

Sing a song of six-pence for your sake,
And drink a bottle full of tory lies,
Four and twenty refugees in a boat,
Just trying to find a life,

They told me a boat sank today,
So what I suggest you just beat them all today,
Knuckle Draggers and Flag Shaggers,
That your poor old granddad,
Had to fight in '36 to deny them.

Trying Political

Trying to write political,
I really haven't got a clue,
Everything I read about,
Is always somebody else's point of view.

I know enough about the Tories,
That's why I'll never vote blue,
I'd love to vote Labour,
But even they don't speak the truth.

Listening to the chimes of Big Ben,
swallowing lies to the beat from number 10.

I know enough to avoid MSM,
Avoid the daily fail,
But lies are spread everywhere,
Looking for truth to no avail.

Massive headlines for us to consume,
Truth buried in nonsense to keep us amused,
Always steering us in a direction,
Trying to guide our views.

Listening to the chimes of Big Ben,
swallowing lies to the beat from number 10.

Can't trust the internet,
Again full of lies,
Conspiracy theories running amok,
Trying to blind our eyes.

Demonising the innocent,
Controlling where to hate,
Tied up in the next thing to have,
Is this really our fate?

(cont)

Listening to the chimes of Big Ben,
swallowing lies to the beat from number 10.

So I guess I'll find my own way,
Seek out my own kind of truth,
Trust in what I know is right,
Hoping my senses don't misconstrue.

Hating those who just cause hurt,
Keep my eyes open on this path,
Ignore the bastards by the Big Ben bell,
I know they just sit and laugh.

Listening to the chimes of Big Ben,
swallowing lies to the beat from number 10.

Me and You

Hello me,
Hello you.

Me is what the world sees,
You are inside and hidden.

Hello you,
Hello me.

You are hiding in the shadows,
Me is loud and running free.

Hello me,
Hello you.

Me is laughing at everything,
You are lost in the madness.

Hello you,
Hello me.

You are a place deep inside,
Me is out there and loud.

Hello me,
Hello you.

Me is a facade,
You are true.

Haunt Their Dream

I don't know where they come from,
There already formed in my head,
The lines just flow on to the paper,
Never knowing how my brain is fed.

Sometimes they are very long,
Sometimes very short,
All freely written,
Hardly edited so it's true thought.

Sometimes there happy and bouncy,
Other times they're full of harm and dread,
Always written unconsciously,
Straight out of my head.

Words words words,
Like a dripping tap they appear,
Sometimes full of love,
Those are dedicated to my dear.

Sometimes live my writing in fear,
What if they don't come, suddenly stop,
What if this stream of nonsense dries up?
I may not be able to continue and that's my lot.

But that day's still not here,
Let my words flow like a river stream,
Hoping they mean something to someone,
Even if they only haunt their dream.

Missiles Of Your Mind

Still falling with this rope twisted round my neck.
Choking my esteem and leaving me empty.
Tiredness taking control of my soul.
Looking for the light shining to cut the ties like a burning flame.

Wrapped up in memories in what should have been said.
Replaying past scenes looking for the clues.
Jumping from past experience like a badly scratched record on a deck.
No following linear with a clearly defined path.

Self-consciously loathing all that can't change.
Like a short circuit finding its own path.
Beating yourself mentally worse than any landed blow.
A messed-up process remembering only the bad words.

Portraying a hard outside which is a thin veneer.
Functional for the world to see, but inside sounding like an out of tune radio.
Burying yourself so deep inside, struggling in your own quicksand.
Vomiting words to disguise your inner turmoil.

Saying the words people need to hear, without hearing them yourself.
Drowning in platitudes and deeds you cannot feel.
Cannons firing past deeds like missiles of your mind.
Still falling with this rope twisted round my neck.

Collar

When you walk in silence with your collar turned up like a shroud,
Hiding from the world because it's far too loud.

No interaction with life's fickle twisting fate,
Hiding from within and without from this world you created and hate.

No understanding from anyone you meet,
They have no idea of the thoughts in your head that make life seem bleak.

Neurodivergent in a world full of sound,
Thought process differences which mean you can't ground.

Wanting interactions of others but not knowing where to begin,
Coming across weird, clumsy and anxious you start to give in.

Like a square peg in the world shaped hole,
Sharp edges instead of a well-rounded whole.
In spite of all this madness I'm here still standing tall,
To those who accept me I love you, to the rest, fuck you all.

Neuro Divergent Head

This is me for every day,
A mixed-up mess in my inner lair,
Sometimes fucked up beyond knowing,
Product of a system of child (less) care.

Now I have got to my 50's,
Slowly learning on how to undo,
Keep on plugging away for answers,
To unlock the past and give it its due.

Still very hard moving forward,
When drilled in your life will be a mess,
Not given clear direction,
Feel like a pawn in a game of chess.

You'd think I'd have learnt by now,
Think I'd know what it is I have to do,
Not easy when your life's foundation,
Was built on misdiagnosis and untruth.

Then like a circle rotating,
It continues around and around,
Until your lost in your own head,
Yourself you continually compound.

Can't see the crap beginning,
Can't find the sorry end,
Spinning all directions in motion,
Every direction your brain says send.

It's like your ID is your universe,
No one else ever can enter,
Caught in self-worth and loathing,
Unable to regulate and centre.

(cont)

Of course people come and go,
Sometimes question if they're even real,
Needing to scream and reach out,
Just so you get a reaction and feel.

It doesn't show on the outside,
You're ok if anyone dare ask,
Your life lived in a tormented masquerade,
Eyes baring your soul behind your mask.

Still Sing Protest Songs

Still the same old sing a long,
Another decade past,
Still sing protest songs.

What's changed, not a lot,
Still tipping our hat,
Still the same old lot.

Yes, it's true,
The colour has changed,
Blue, red then back to blue.

Still we sing and moan,
Saying we want change,
But still your vote condones.

Now we have social media,
Still keeping us shackled,
With tik tok to feed ya.

It's not working.

Time to take to the street,
Words are not enough,
Time to take it to the street.

Another year has rolled on,
No more looking backwards,
Time to move on.

Write your placards and sign,
Direct action,
Now is the time.

(cont)

No more living on scraps were fed,
No more hoping the next lot will be better,
Time to claim it back before we're dead.
We were the generation that was meant to change,
What ever happened to us,
But I look around it's still the same.

This is our last chance,
It's worse than before,
Time to make a stance.

It's 's not working.

Time to take to the street,
Words are not enough,
Time to take it to the street.

Stood In My Garden

The darkness of night,
Stood in my garden.

The silence is deafening,
Stood in my garden.

Stars just breaking through the cloud,
Stood in my garden.

Only noise is my breath,
Stood in my garden.

The wind lazily rustling the trees,
Stood in my garden.

A sound of an animal burrowing,
Stood in my garden.

Just taking in the night,
Stood in my garden.

Not everything needs a reason,
Stood in my garden.

The chill of the night air,
Stood in my garden.

Minutes turning to hours,
Stood in my garden.

It's the simplest things that are good for the soul,
Stood in my garden.

King of the Toast

I used to boast,
I made the best toast,
The one you adored,
You wanted it most.

The bread was perfection,
A glorious golden,
It was up there with the masters,
Wonderful to beholden.

It was talked about in whispers,
Across the land it was admired,
Even the Michelin chefs,
My toast they just desired.

The butter was spread so evenly,
Across the toast it gleams,
The perfect correct ratio,
The toast of your dreams.

The jam was the final part,
Spread adoringly across the top,
It was the height of brilliance,
My toast skills could not stop.

But then it came crashing down,
I left it to long a minor slip,
The darkest burnt toast you ever saw,
My reputation ruined for a slight blip.

So the moral of this story is,
Don't make toast when you're tired,
You're only as good as the last slice made,
From my toast duty, sadly I was fired.

Not The Same

Hate being away from you,
Texts and calls aren't the same,
Sending you love songs,
Because the separation hurts my brain.

Counting the hours,
Each one passing so old,
Needing your warm embrace,
It's like I'm missing my soul.

Can't stand this emptiness,
Like my being is torn in two,
Days dragging like weeks,
I'm so missing you.

Missing our normal routine,
Just the silly things we do,
Missing our cuddles,
Missing hearing 'I love you'.

Mark Wants a Banjo

Mark wants a banjo,
But Lee said no,
Now me and Rod have no place to practice,
Nowhere to go.

Mark wants a banjo,
Accused me and Rod of fueling,
So it will unlikely happen,
No Banjos there for dueling.

Mark wants a banjo,
To go with his collection of guitars,
But he knows which side his bread buttered,
Better than having to sleep in his car.

Mark wants a banjo,
But his dream has floundered,
What Lee doesn't know is me and Rod,
Are going to get this crowd funded.

Mark wants a banjo,
I want to hear him play it at gigs,
I'm sure he'll knock awesome tunes out,
So we can all dance a little jig.

Mark wants a banjo,
Oh Lee, hear his cry,
And as long as there is social media,
Me and Rod won't let this die.

Gammon Bloke

Heterosexual car owners on caffeine.
Driving big cars to hide their insecurities.

Just an extension to cover small penises.
The straightest person you'll ever meet.

To hear them talk, like their bollocks hang down by their feet.
Not sure of sexuality in case they seem weak.

Shout the loudest at sports events with thinly veiled racist rant.
Put on your best hard man accent call everyone a "cant".
" Oi you, you fuckin' prick, what the hell ya want."

Go drink some Stella, become a drunk preacher.
Go home hit the missus you wife beater.

"Serves the slag right, that'll teach her."
Read your daily mail as if it's a bible.

Closed to all that don't agree and they stifle.
"Wouldn't have put up with it in the past, I'd shoot them with a rifle."

What a bunch of tossers afraid to be woke,
Don't even understand what it means that's the joke,
Just in case they come across as not a gammon bloke.

The People Should Start Revolting

When your mind is full of hunger,
And your stomach is racked in pain,
When you're working long hours,
Choosing food, over heating,
The fucking Tories are to blame.

When you're working, using food banks,
Just to feed your own,
The prices are increasing,
Under the Tories food debt has grown.

The people should start revolting,
And the government moan,
Fight the fucking overlords,
Beat them in their homes.

When you're waiting for the ambulance,
It's not the workers fault so don't blame them,
Underfunded over worked NHS failing,
The fucking Tories are to blame.

When you can't afford fuel to go to work,
Remember whose causing this,
The pump prices keep increasing
The fucking Tories caused this.

The people should start revolting,
And the government moan,
Fight the fucking overlords,
Beat them in their homes.

When you're paying high rents,
Can't find no place to live,
Shit hole slums for rent,
The Tory landlords condone this.

When you're crawling through the gutter,
Just another peasant in this race,
The fucking government make the rules,
Just to keep you in your place.

The people should start revolting,
And the government moan,
Fight the fucking overlords,
Beat them in their homes.

The people should start revolting,
And the government moan,
Fight the fucking overlords,
Beat them in their homes.

The people should start revolting,
And the government moan,
Fight the fucking overlords,
Beat them in their homes.

Controlled TV

Cheap entertainment to keep the masses amused,
Media fed junkies, waiting for their fix shuffling in shoes.

Getting their controlled banality fix of reality TV,
Not realising they're brainwashed with no hope to be free.

Living for their chance at Warhol effect,
Soul sold for 15 minutes, forever in debt.

Always forever chasing that game fed need,
Now just lost in the gutter from the machine they feed,
Blinkered forever from reality and what they could see,
Always chasing that lost adoration, that is the price paid fee.

As Chumbawamba once said.

'Flickering pictures hypnotise,
We spend our life watching others' lives,
Too much watching to realise,
That this is a smokescreen,
And this is why people die.'

White Soap Powder

It wasn't my fault,
It's just history,
All in the past,
I'll just wash my hands,
Use that new white soap powder,
It's called White Wash.

Me and my black mate walked into a bar,
We just blue dyed our hair,
Oh look at him with the blue hair,
Oh look at the black bloke with the blue hair,
Not look at those two with blue hair,
See it's already inbred and there.

Ok I lied, I haven't got any Mates,
I just used it to prove my point,
The fact I had to tell you it was a black mate says we have to go far,
My skin isn't a barrier built on misconception,
But that's white privilege for ya.

We need to look at the language we use,
Black circa 13th century,
Soiled or stained with dirt,
This is just the starting seed,
Negative leading to hurt.

Then roll on the 1580's,
A new meaning to add,
Dark or deadly purposes,
Only at the beginning makes me mad.

(cont)

Black Soul, wicked or atrocious,
Black Augury, evil divination of the flight of birds,
Feeling any ownership yet,
The list goes on it's absurd.
17th and 18th Century,
Let's add more to the list,
Sorrow, melancholy, gloom and dire,
No wonder people are pissed.

Black Guard, a dirty shabby fellow,
Black Mail, protection bribery money,
Black Sheep, a bad person,
It goes on it's not funny,
Black listed, disgrace or censure,
I can list lots but will miss my point.

Don't be afraid to own up to it,
White privilege isn't said to cause hate.

It's there to make you think,
It's there because we made it,
It's there to make you change,
It's there because it's an invisible barrier,
It's there when police are profiling,
It's there when walking a street,
It's there at job interviews,
It's there when your kids date,
It's there when you walk into a bank,
It's there when you watch the news,
It's just fucking everywhere.

We need to educate ourselves,
We deserve to bow in shame,
We deserve the blame.
We can't say it was in the past,
We can't say it was nothing to do with me,
We can't say I'm not to blame,
Why, because we carry that white privilege built on the past.

Our colonial past created this problem,
It's up to us to fix it.
Bright white shining light,
Pitch black I cannot see,
It's ingrained in our language,
That's plain to see,
A massive blight from history.

I don't want a part of it wasn't my fault,
It's just history,
All in the past,
I'll just wash my hands,
Use that new white soap powder,
It's called White Wash.

We don't need to be a part of it wasn't my fault,
It's just history,
All in the past,
I'll just wash my hands,
Use that new white soap powder,
It's called White Wash.

We need to acknowledge
It was our fault,
We created this history,
It's not all in the past,
I will not wash my hands,
I won't use that new white soap powder,
It's called White Wash.

I Believe

I believe in hurricanes,
your life will not be the same,
everything is open to change.

I believe in changing fate,
Don't have to be first in this race,
Everyone has their own pace.

I believe in the totality of love,
Once found it is enough,
But hold onto it nothing lasts for good.

I believe in great friends,
Who will always be there to mend,
With thoughts of positivity to send.

I believe you should eat good food,
When confronted with the menu brood,
Tasting great can heighten your mood.

I believe in the patter of falling rain,
Turn your head upwards cleanse your soul,
Looking at your life, prioritise your goal.

I believe there is sunshine after the dark,
When the black dog appears with his pack,
We reach out, we holler and send him back.

I believe in playing music loud,
We sing and shout and dance,
We feel good and jump and prance.

I believe in the moment of living now,
Our tomorrows are not guaranteed,
Do it all today and be happy and pleased.

I believe in being true to yourself,
You may not always be right,
But in the end, it all turns out alright.

I believe in the miracle of birth,
There is nothing to compare to this,
A life you created brings such bliss.

I believe in doing things that scare,
Fight off your demons and take the chance,
We only have this life so take a stance.

I believe in all of life,
Don't judge others without knowing,
This is how we learn and continue growing.

I believe in fighting for what's right,
Never be rolled over or out to shame,
Beat down on wrongness and sometimes accept blame.

I believe in taking long walks,
Sometimes it's good for solace and be in your head,
Sorting problems out, keep your brain fed.

I believe in me and you,
Together we can be ourselves,
Not hiding like a forgotten relic, hidden on a shelf.

I believe in the words I write,
I hope sometimes they move things in you,
I hope they make you think and look for what's true.

Hello

Hello meltdown my old friend,
Come to fuck my life again,
Like an invasion in my brain,
Not chance for clear thought,
Just here to cause pain.

Revert backwards to past behaviour,
Not even consciously aware,
Done without any thought,
Not even a flash across your brain,
You could get caught in this loop again.

Then that bit eventually passes,
It's like a sudden reality,
Shit what happened again,
Whatever have I done I don't recall,
Meltdowns are in no shape or form fun.

Lost only in instant reaction,
Looped in anger and frustration again,
Like a constant looping sound wave,
Like a never-ending train,
Like a warped and out of control brain.

See Myself for Real

I'm a law unto myself,
Constantly dreaming.

Chance to change and bypass things,
Constantly scheming.

See myself for real,
See myself for real.

Got a misfired mind,
An unchained brain,
To change my life,
Not live-in refrain.

Take a path that might be wrong,
Constantly feeling.

Never will know if you stay safe and warm,
Constantly changing.

See myself for real,
See myself for real.

Got a misfired mind,
An unchained brain,
To change my life,
Not live-in refrain.

Running down the wrong life path,
Constantly convincing.

Getting comfortable and throwing it away,
Constantly disturbing.

(cont)

Got a misfired mind,
An unchained brain,
To change my life,
Not live-in refrain.

See myself for real,
(Whilst hiding inside),
See myself for real,
(Whilst hiding inside).

So take my hand and running free,
Jump into the void, come drown with me.

Leave the cares behind, heavy in the dirt,
Roundabout rewinding, recoiling from hurt.

Back to the beginning, come start again,
Forge a new way forward, unlink that chain.

Got a misfired mind,
An unchained brain,
To change my life,
Not live-in refrain.

See myself for real,
(Whilst hiding inside),
See myself for real,
(Whilst hiding inside).

See myself for real.

Prime Control

The worlds gone barking mad,
It isn't even sublime,
Queuing for flavoured water,
The YouTube led Prime.

Adults pushing kids,
Have we really come to this?
Fighting in the supermarket aisle,
Over a bottle of flavoured piss.

Can't believe the sight,
People trampled under feet,
Just because an influencer led it,
The masses swallow it like sheep.

Do we no longer care,
Are we really in a world of greed,
Led by Logan Paul and KSI,
Feeding people a new dog lead.

It's just bloody water,
Bit of coconut thrown in on top,
Then stuff you can get from Multivitamins,
This consumer crap has got to stop.

I don't have time for influencers,
Paid by corporations to lead the sheeple,
It's time the blinkers were removed,
Time to realise we are people.

With all the wrong in the world,
Just another example of bad social media,
Just more brainwashing people control,
Just more to hide the truth and lead you.

(cont)

While we're being blindsided,
Subliminal guidance under our roof,
The power again of the controlling leaders,
To keep you amused and away from truth.

So give it a few more weeks,
Will be something new to take its place,
The next must have thing,
To keep you as a rat tied to this race.

Your Eyes

When I look in your eyes,
Keep me safe from a world I despise.

Feel your kisses on my lips,
Warmth flows through me, I know this is it.

To be with you fully, found you at last,
Making all the pain worthwhile I accumulated from my past.

You're like my Angel who has come from above,
To keep me safe, surrounded by your love.

A Simple Love Piece

The words are simple to make it clear,
Let you know my feelings are real,
You're not a passing infatuation,
No words can express how I feel.

I could write the world's best love poem,
I could play you love songs for ever,
I could shout it out for eternity,
If I could that would be my endeavour.

I look into your eyes,
Get pulled deep into your soul,
Just to stay there in your heart,
Sends my mind out of control.

To hold you while you're sleeping,
Having your warmth next to me,
Know that my soul is caught forever,
Trapped, never wanting to be free.

I bet you didn't know,
You hook me with your smile,
Just the little things,
The way you dress, your style.

My Twee Weepy Left Tit

It started with scrabble,
Making words that can fit,
I couldn't believe the placed tiles,
Spelt 'My Twee Weepy Left Tit'.

So ensued the discussion,
What this statement could mean,
Is it a proper clinical condition?
Or just random words it seems.

So out with medical dictionary,
To see what we could find,
Wondering what is this infliction,
That could blight mankind.

Is it an important issue?
That can inflict regardless of gender,
Is it more common to age bands?
It's a complete mind bender.

So if you are suffering,
Please disregard my wit,
I'm so sorry that you suffer from,
'My Twee Weepy Left Tit'.

12-12-22

This is it, ASD day,
The culmination of your past,
Was it just you being naughty?
Is it the key to unlock your angst?

Why was you put in care?
Why do you have meltdowns?
Why do you withdraw from those you love?
Why do you know so much about nothing?
Why do you put on so many different faces?
Why do you talk at the most inappropriate moments?
Why do you feel so overwhelmed with emotions?
Why do you show lack of emotions?
Why do you look like you don't care?
Why do you not go out much?
Why do you try so hard?
Why do you hide away?
Just Why?

I hope this brings you some answers, even if it's to that one burning question, Why?

Well I've walked through the door,
But just want to turn back,
So hate this feeling of anxiety,
It's like a chimp stuck on my back.

So I've buried my head in this,
My words just there to assure,
This is what I'm fighting for,
Just something to self-reassure.

Is it all lies am I just like that,
Will I get any answers for?
My life, or should I say lack,
Just waiting for answers, claim myself back.

(cont)

So now the clock is ticking,
My appointments already late,
Just sat here now in self-loathing,
God my life I sometimes hate.

Can't believe I'm doing it,
Someone who doesn't know me to analyse,
But I'm holding on to what my ex-partner said,
I know this is my life lol.

Well there you go,
It's took 54 years but finally done,
You now have answers for your past,
You're Autistic Son.

But wait there I've not finished,
I've got more news you see,
I've also come to the conclusion,
It's more, you also have ADHD.

So there it is,
A conclusion on my past,
I now have the answers too,
I just wasn't a naughty kid in my past.

Even now, each day I go through,
I now have an answer to why I'm not like you,
It's not that I'm not bothered and don't care,
It's I process things differently so can seem unaware.

Please Be Direct

It's not easy being neuro divergent,
Don't always read things right,
Sometimes even the slightest words said,
Just little things, can keep me up all night.

Did I really get that right?
I haven't at times got a clue,
Left working out what it meant,
Sometimes I don't know what to do.

Even the simplest things,
They have to be 100% spelled out,
If there's room for interpretation,
Yep, I'll be pondering that alright.

Sometimes you just need to be direct,
Spell it out right down to the letter,
Otherwise my brain gets locked out,
Leaves me wondering which choice is better.

I don't choose to do it this way,
Even if at times it can annoy you,
Just need it telling straight,
That's all I ask of you.

For James

Don't die with the music inside you,
Follow the beat of your life,
Like a rhythm through your body,
Like the centre of your hive.

Beats spiraling outward,
Chapter of your life a new verse,
Captured in the moments,
Joining in with your voice.

Lost in the tune,
Each one with its own stance,
Pounding and beating,
Lost in the perpetual dance.

Marking your memories,
As you step along the course,
Love, joy and hopefulness,
Anger, bitterness and remorse.

The music covers every emotion,
A page bookmarked in our head,
But better to mark it with sound,
As we weave our own thread.

The Void

See you there taking a look at me,
Thinking you know my whole history.

Come take a journey, it won't take long,
Everything you know about me is wrong.

I fed you my edited story like a book,
The expurgated version, bits I let you look.

Chapters and pages kept hidden away,
Glad I did because our trust went today.

So tell the world your skewed story of me,
Only half the facts presented for all to see.

Stabbing at me with your sharp verbal knife,
I'm so glad I edited you, from parts of my life.

With your repeated unfounded half-truths,
Decorating lies, like bunting from a roof.

Knew it was inside you, ready to shout out,
Don't even know what you're shouting about.

The story is getting quite old and it's boring,
I'm surprised the audience aren't snoring.

I'm so glad it's gone, I can no longer feel,
Like our whole relationship was so unreal.

I've moved so far on from the past,
It's like you're there still trying to grasp.

It's done and finished, now it's just noise,
Can't wait for the silence to fill in the void.

The Beginning

Started life so young,
Whilst my peers were still learning,
Bored with that already,
I needed more in the dawn of my morning.

Not happy with 75 matchboxes,
They did not stimulate my brain,
Too young to know what I wanted,
Just knew life was a drain.

Standing out away from my peers,
Not joining in the so-called fun games,
But curiously interested in the interaction,
The fallouts, name calling and blame.

Sat in the classroom bored,
Nothing new there to absorb,
Happy in my own little world,
Just playing the game like a chore.

So old in young shoes,
Sounds like a cliche,
But it's not, it's my life,
Bored without and within me.

No one asking are you ok,
No one there to listen or guide,
So closed myself from the outside world,
Just happy with me inside.

But still those external pressures,
Teachers saying do things this way,
Never asking what I really wanted,
No wonder I wasn't ok.

So branded as disinterested,
A trouble maker to be sure,
Just someone to mock and laugh at,
As I screamed and beat the floor.

It didn't get any better,
With no one really there,
Isolated in my own little box,
Wrapped up and dressed, bundled into care.

The Dog Joke One

Where's the dog gone?
He disappeared from the park,
Can't see his nodding head,
Or hear his distinctive bark.

You should look 'Harder',
That's what my missus said to me,
So I took her words on board,
I've got a plan just wait and see.

First trip is off to the barbers,
Shave my head is what I'll do,
Then it's time to build some muscle,
Then of to get inked a nice big tattoo.

So now I look much much harder,
I still haven't found the damn dog,
Also got sacked in the meantime,
My new look doesn't suit my job.

Two Words Two Views

Words hurt,
Stares cut,
Lies belittle,
Truth blinds,
People bind,
Life flows,
Trust goes,
Love hurts,
Tears grow,
Unwinding no,
Backwards go.

Start again,
New fresh,
Full life,
Smile jest,
Tickle laugh,
New path,
Green grass,
People laugh,
News flash,
Learning grow,
Togetherness flow.

They Shall Not Pass

Pepper bags at horses' noses,
Marbles rolling at their feet,
Mounted police are falling,
Black shirts will never march our street.

Turn over the collected lorries,
Barriers covered with slabs,
Block up the entrances and alleys,
We will let no fascist pass.

Stand with the east end together,
With fists raised high as one,
Defending from the barricades,
Turn back the black shirt scum.

We will amass where they gather,
Each of us all ready to fight,
To stand as one together,
Chants of 'No Pasaran' we unite.

So wherever the Mosley type gather,
Even today in the reform disguise,
We will never forget our history,
You, you fascist who we despise.

On every October the 4th,
We must never ever forget,
To still beat down on fascists,
We must keep that ideology dead.

Always we will unite together,
No matter our creed or class,
Like the chant echoing from 1936,
'They shall not pass'.

Exit The Cage

I will not be silenced,
My voice will be heard,
My words have a life,
Not caged like a bird.

I will not be silenced,
My voice will be heard,
My words have a life,
Not caged like a bird.

You may not like my history,
Distort it with lies,
No longer damage me,
That I despise.

I have had my issues,
I own them it's true,
But life changes,
It's not up to you.

I've carved a new path,
A new journey true,
I have no time for hatred,
My futures not you.

You may try to blight me,
Put obstacles in the way,
But I will rise higher than mountains,
Each step taking me further away.

Whoever you think I am,
You never knew me inside,
Lost in your opinion,
Buried from the inside.

I'd forgot who I was,
Lost my sense of worth,
Finally emerging from shackles,
But finally I'm free and set forth.

I will not be silenced,
My voice will be heard,
My words have a life,
Not caged like a bird.

I will not be silenced,
My voice will be heard,
My words have a life,
Not caged like a bird.

Puppet

Well that's just changed the narrative,
With placed words you said,
Mouthpiece for others,
Not words from your head.

Like little word bombs,
Destroying all in its path,
But you not understanding,
Just used for a spiteful laugh.

Lies for reasons,
With just a pinch of fact,
Just trying to silence me,
This is your act.

Used just like a puppet,
A pathway to me,
I wish your puppet master,
Could just set you free.

But while I'm still standing,
Just living my life,
Use you as a puppet,
To attack like a knife.

Lies for reasons,
With just a pinch of fact,
Just trying to silence me,
This is your act.

I will not falter,
I never will fall,
Each beat down I'm stronger,
I'll outwill you all.

I'm already damaged,
Shame you can't see,
I carry my scars inwardly,
You'll never beat me.

Lies for reasons,
With just a pinch of fact,
Just trying to silence me,
This is your act.

Lest We Forget

As the grass now grows,
The red poppies dance,
Come down to Flanders Field,
Here the silence of the dance.

No longer the sound,
Screaming artillery overhead,
No more mud-covered trenches,
No more sweethearts to mourn the dead,
No longer the gas clouds,
No more whistles to blow,
No more over the top,
Only the red poppies grow.

No more anguish or pain,
Seeing comrades as they bled,
No more buried alive in trenches,
No more sweethearts to mourn the dead,
No longer the gas clouds,
No more whistles to blow,
No more over the top,
Only the red poppies grow.

No longer to be heard,
The chattering machine gun dread,
No more Pals slaughtered,
No more sweethearts to mourn the dead,
No longer the gas clouds,
No more whistles to blow,
No more over the top,
Only the red poppies grow.

As the grass now grows,
The red poppies dance,
Come down to Flanders Field,
Here the silence of the dance.

Stay Grounded

Going to try to regulate,
Not sure what to do,
Thought I could face anything,
But that came out the blue.

I'm like are you serious,
Is this an actual joke,
Is this even reality,
Better give my ribs a poke.

I can't explain it,
Have no idea why,
Can't even place it,
No matter how I try.

But now I've been tripped over,
Teetering on the fence,
Dark feelings taking over,
Thinking too much, trying to make sense.

So now I'm another room,
Just need time on my own,
Not nice I now feel outside,
Whilst still inside our home.

Can't tell you how I'm feeling,
Wouldn't know where to start,
On top of everything else today,
This just breaks my heart.

I'm not sure how to handle this,
We've had no real problems before,
Always me and you together,
But now my feelings on the floor.

(cont)

I don't know what you're feeling,
Too scared to even come back,
Just hiding beyond your reach,
Waiting patiently for the sack.

Does it seem weird to you?
That I'm sat here close, but far away,
Trying to keep myself grounded,
To try to regulate in my own way.

I'm not very sociable,
When I'm feeling like this,
Cut myself off from you,
When all I want is to cuddle and kiss.

Reflected Reality

What if the person in the mirror is the real me?
What if I'm the reflection living in the shadows.

Just filling in time till I return to the mirror,
Just to stand for moments mimicking their pose.

What if I am the other side of the looking glass,
Slowly becoming self-aware this is just moments.

Could any of this be an actual reality,
After all I'm always ready in time to be at the mirror.

I'm always in the right place and time,
To be shown to my other self never late.

Could you imagine the shock to my other self?
Just once if I escaped and was never there.

Not sure it would ever happen not to appear,
But just once it would be nice not to be the reflection.

Self-Entitled

It's a shame when diversity is hidden,
With nothing visual to compare,
Because you can't see it,
Don't dismiss it, like it's not there.

Do people need to carry a placard,
Hoisted high for all to see,
Or perhaps a voice recording,
Shouting " Hidden Disability".

The reality is we should need neither,
It's just this day and age,
But in a world of social media,
Like idiots freed from a cage.

You have your keyboard warriors,
Whose only sense of worth,
Is to always belittle strangers,
Regardless of pain or hurt.

Then it carries into daily life,
With no real morals to self-check,
In a world full of just about you,
Like you're the only card in the deck.

It's not the way life should be,
Constant entitled cries of its not fair,
Nobody looking out for each other,
In a world that no longer cares.

We've forgotten social interaction,
With things we shout and say,
Forgotten basic humanity,
This is the new world order today.

Frozen Raspberries and Pineapple

Frozen raspberries and pineapple,
It really is the simple things,
I could give you diamonds,
Yes, they're nice,
Fur Coats, well maybe faux fur,
DMs by the dozen,
In a multitude of colours,
Dior and Chanel,
Till you smell of sweet Paris,
Cruises round the world,
Be the princess of the sea,
A Bentley or Rolls Royce,
A Bugatti that goes so fast,
Fine dine you in the Ivy,
But frozen raspberries and pineapple,
It really is the simple things that last.

Bubbles

Floating like bubbles,
In my stirred coffee cup,
Waiting for the moment,
To spin and pop,
Relentlessly spinning,
In a world that will not stop,
Caught in a teaspoon whirlpool,
Drowning in hot liquid,
But still like the bubbles,
Floating to the top,
Never drowning,
Just constantly rising,
Until the fateful explosion,
When you no longer exist,
The world just stops.

Shut The Fuck Up

Shut the fuck up,
My nightly cry,
Watching the TV,
With your noise beside.
Oh Joe really,
What you doing to me,
Shut the fuck up,
I'm trying to sleep.
You know I'm not nasty,
I only mean you well,
Shut the fuck up,
You're a chattering hell.
I can't believe it,
You're like a young pup,
Even cuddled together,
Shut the fuck up.
Shut the fuck up,
It's the middle of the night,
Feel like suffocating you with a pillow,
That will give you a fright.
You know I don't mean it,
We have a loving cup,
But just do me a favour,
Shut the fuck up.

Farts Innit

Farting under the covers,
You have no idea how it felt,
To smell your putrid guff,
It seemed to make my face melt.

Then you did the ultimate sin,
Pulled the duvet over my head,
Lay there spluttering and choking,
Never knew if I would end up dead.

What the hell have you eaten,
Making me suffer all this pain,
Like a dead rat stuck up your arse,
Like sewage flowing out the drain.

How can someone so beautiful,
Release this deadly toxic cloud,
Should carry a Health warning,
People could die in your fart shroud.

I really think it's very wrong,
I do seriously ought to mention,
I'm sure there is a paragraph about you,
It's there in the Geneva Convention.

Nameless Face

To live on the edge of society,
Classed as an outsider,
Not fitting in to the expected norms,
A nameless face, not realising your ambitions are wider.

Ignored at every opportunity,
Unable to pass through the turnstile,
Disappearing inside your own clothes,
A nameless face, with a sardonic smile.

Just a number on a piece of paper,
Another body to join the social queue,
Keep shuffling slowly forward,
A nameless face, sign here as you always do.

It's the justification bi weekly chore,
Having to justify your decision and choice,
I've been applying here's my log,
A nameless face, repeated mantra from your voice.

We are a caring government,
You're sick of hearing that drone,
Lies running faster than truth,
A nameless face, caught in their monotone.

Round and round in circles,
This is how the charade continues to grow,
With nonexistent opportunities,
A nameless face, with nowhere else to go.

But still you keep on hanging in,
There will come a moment a purge,
Dreams and ambition pushing forward,
A nameless face, purified ready to surge.

Time to stand as one together,
Fist raised high and ready to fight,
Time to show this wasting government,
A nameless face, altogether unite.

Boris, Fucked My Barbecue

Boris, fucked my barbecue,
I still remember it now,
The fire engine has such a distinctive howl,
I didn't want a burnt burger bun,
But I was glued to the telly,
Watching the count, such fun,

I lamented at my ruined corn on the cob,
But it was far to riveting,
Watching people resign from their job.
It got out of hand,
I ruined my fish,
Watching the mass exodus,
It was all pretty swish.

Destroyed my spatula,
Totally wrecked it,
But I was listening to him go,
But at least he did Brexit.
It was my fault it spread,
It set fire to the forest,
But it was worth it,
To see the demise of Boris.

5 & 6

Weird to comprehend at five you know you don't fit,
Looking at your peer group knowing you're on the fringe,
Not having the same interests as you see them as boring,
School days were a school daze every minute passing like an hour.

Not bothered what adventures Peter and Jane are up to,
Yearning for learning not the stuff I already knew,
Retreating inside my own mind trying to become invisible in the class,
Much happier in a world of make believe and dreams.

Already bucking a school system that just seemed irrelevant,
Not caring about the popular tunes and whose number one,
Disdainfully looking at Shang-a-lang and the obligatory tartan inserts,
Trying to find my place in an ever-changing world.

Always bucking at rules that seemed to just chain me,
All this already clear at five and dreading the path laid out,
Walking round like a square peg being forced into a round hole,
Trying desperately to be heard but treated as voiceless.

Everyone telling me what I should be to fit to conform,
Asking me questions but not accepting my answers,
So aware already at five I just became disenchanted and restless,
Is this really the path we all follow behind the Judas goat?

I did try to fit in, become part of the accepted norm,
But my heart wasn't in it I only knew how to be me,
Then whisked away at six to be put in care and hidden from view,
Threatened with punishment and sometimes violence.

All for being different and not conforming, just being me,
All for not fitting into the established education mould,
All sold to my family like a Blyton adventure story,
Six was definitely a change but not for the better.

For Mark

Now another year has passed,
I hope your feeling wiser,
You're such a smashing bloke,
A one hundred percent top geezer.

Love to the posts you do,
On moths and all the food,
Although I've not had a dinner invite,
I know you're not being rude.

I love the t-shirts you model,
They really are quite Ace,
Even if most of them,
Are displaying your beautiful face.

I hope this year brings you everything,
Full of love and all that's fine,
So have a brilliant day and year,
I'll catch you soon down the 'Frontline'.

Dishy Rishi

Oh dishy Rishi,
Our new saviour,
At last he's found,
Oh dishy Rishi,
We will never forget that,
You fucked up the pound.

Oh dishy Rishi,
You've arrived,
Got here in time,
Oh dishy Rishi,
Shall we forget,
You also were convicted of crime.

Oh dishy Rishi,
The world will remember,
Just wait and see,
Oh dishy Rishi,
How you fleeced the coffers,
Contracts to buddies for PPE.

Oh dishy Rishi,
Just smile at us,
Beam that false reassurance,
Oh dishy Rishi,
I'll give it a week before,
You reverse the cut on National Insurance.

Oh dishy Rishi,
The time has come,
Now time to face a fact,
Oh dishy Rishi,
Questions of non-dom status,
Are you going to pay that tax?

Oh dishy Rishi,
It's like it was written,
Your god given fate,
Oh dishy Rishi,
For those who mourned alone,
We remember Party gate.

Oh dishy Rishi,
There's plenty here,
We will remind,
Oh dishy Rishi,
We will carry on,
Till we're rid of your kind.

As You Have Gone

As you have gone,
Your journey through the sand,
Know you was my rock,
Always my guiding hand.

Let me take the burden,
Be the strength now you've gone,
I will keep the flame burning,
Shine your love on everyone.

I know times won't be easy,
But within me, you're still there,
Every day I will praise you,
Show the world how much I care.

I will keep our laughter going,
Keep our humour through the days,
Remember each time I hurt I'm alive,
Deep ingrained into me, one of our ways.

Larry Cat PM

It's happened we now have Larry,
Stop politics becoming a bore,
A cat ruling from number 10,
Giving more than those gone before.

A ruling all doors push button,
This is the first new law,
Cats don't have opposable thumbs,
Meowing waiting for humans is such a chore.

Next, it's the average day,
23 hours to stay in bed,
Apart from feeding and grooming,
That's why we have the hour, Larry said.

Seaside beaches declared litter trays,
With the tide to wash it away,
Larry said it shouldn't be a problem,
It's where we already put our shit today.

To immediately ban the fracking,
We don't need the extra gas,
Larry says the best way to keep warm,
Is to nod vigorously while licking our ass.

No more number 10 waifs and strays,
It's driving Larry quite mad,
He's so sorry he can no longer pity them,
There so fucking stupid it's make him sad.

He's let in a pig fucker,
He let in one whose a clown,
Then he let in a mark 2 Thatcherite,
He wished he'd let it drown.

So now he's had enough,
Middle claw up and tail unfurled,
Quick statement 'you're all my bitches now',
Larry's in charge, welcome to cat world.

See You

See you,
My breath skips,
Hear you,
My mind flips,
Touch you,
I'm in a whirl,
Feel you,
I'm holding my girl,
Taste you,
Sweet and like salt,
You you,
Got hold of my heart.

Sweat

you're making me sweat, Full of regret,
Can't believe you think I'm still under your influence.

Striking out alone, deleted you from my phone, Clarity to think and my thoughts just my own.

Time and time just the same, noise in my brain, your constant control drove me insane.

Like an everlasting water drip, just behind my eyes, welled up with hatred, it's you I despise.

Where You Came From

Remember where you came from,
The things you stood for,
Wheels are turning full circle,
We've all been here before.

Thatcherism in a Truss,
A mimic of the past,
But still the same old values,
Downtrodden working class.

So time again to rise,
We've beaten this before,
But together we must unite,
To fight of the Tory Whore.

They will try to control the media,
Brainwash us to turn against each other,
But we must stand together stronger,
As one, with our fellow sister and brother.

We must not blame the striking workers,
They who have no choice but to picket,
Time has come to unite as one for society,
As has gone before, we are all caught in it.

Rising living costs to generate the profits,
All for the top echelons wallets to thicken,
Feed us on just enough scraps, lies and untruths,
Hoping we swallow it, like a grateful chicken.

The government only pretend to care for us,
The colours Red, Green, Yellow and Blue,
It's all just mingled messed up together now,
We need another path, one that's true.

The time is here to stand together,
We the masses must group and unite,
It's time to end this bloody madness,
It's time to gather, stand up and fight.

Bad Addiction

Got a bad addiction,
I put it down to my condition,
I just scratch and scratch my legs,
Until there are scars from where I bled,
I thought it was anxiety,
That was leading to my itch,
But it isn't, it's some other fucking bitch.

Where Did the Words Go?

Years gone by and almost written nothing.
What happened Joe?
Where did the words go?
Were you repressed?
Were you helpless?
Did you lose your way?
Maybe you thought you was happy?
Maybe you thought you'd found love?
Maybe you tried to be different for someone else?
Perhaps the words remained and you got lost?
Was it worth the silence?
Was it worth the cost?
Sometimes the words came to visit, or did I visit them?
I'm not so sure anymore.
I missed the words, I'm glad I got them back again.

Make Your Bed in the Morning

Always make your bed in the morning,
It closes the chapter on yesterday,
Forget about success or failure,
It's a blank page to start today.

Brush your teeth when you get up,
It washes the dirt away,
Nothing left clinging on,
A mouthwash invigorating day.

Put on clean underwear daily,
No one needs to carry yesterday's shit,
It's better to change regularly,
The past is past, that's it.

Privileged Piss

It's not even hidden anymore,
It's there in plain sight,
The disdain for the unwealthy,
The unwelcoming, the working class.
We have millionaires telling us how to budget,
They'll never understand that need,
Giving us grants for fuel poverty,
That go straight to the fuel mongers.
Windfall tax my arse,
It's just a way to launder public money,
But still the people will swallow it,
Just another bitter pill.
How long till we learn,
Those above just piss on below,
Wringing in the drench,
Privileged Piss on us all.

Alone

I'm all alone,
Sat here still waiting,
Watching things pass me by,
Still contemplating.

Words written down,
Some have meaning,
Some are like diarrhoea,
Constantly streaming.

Some are about love,
Some are about hate,
Some are of the past,
Some describe my fate.

Written on happy emotions,
Written in dark days,
All a mixed reflection,
All fogged in a mind haze.

Take this one,
It's shared as it is written,
No structure to what's going on,
I couldn't even be bothered to rhyme this.

It's all just garbage,
It's just words with no thought,
No real meaning,
Just basics I've been taught.

(cont)

I'm no Paul Simmonds or Swill Odgers,
I don't give my words enough thought,
It's as they come out of my head,
Typed out and finally caught.

I just live-in hope,
That the odd one makes a mark,
Stirs some emotions up,
In someone's beating heart.

Your World

Your world,
My world,
Holding each other in the dark.

Your world,
My world,
Keeping safe each other's heart.

Your world,
My world,
Two lovers together in the rain.

Your world,
My world,
Helping each other heal past pain.

Your world,
My world,
Lazy days together lying-in bed.

Your world,
My world,
Making memories forever in our head.

Your world,
My world,
Filling each other up with hope.

Your world,
My world,
Sharing strength when we need to cope.

Your world,
My world,
Seeing clear through all the haze.

(cont)

Your world,
My world,
Holding each other up on dark days.

Your world,
My world,
Sharing our life together as one.

Your world,
My world,
Love that will never be gone.

Ginger Cat

I saw something strange today,
A ginger cat, caught in a tree,
To you, that might not seem strange,
But that ginger cat was me.

About Time

Worse thing about me is time,
Give me a day's plan,
Please don't change it,
Even unforeseen circumstances,
Get hold of my mind and drain it.

Don't arrange to go and all that takes,
Then you tell me it's changed and we're not,
Then it's back on plans have changed,
Then it's not, then it is, this needs to stop.

Don't keep giving me times,
Then there all subject to change,
You have no idea of time OCD,
Wrapped up in an autistic brain.

Then don't have a go at me,
Just because I get anxious and can't cope,
Next, you'll be telling me I'm an adult,
To man up, might as well give me a rope.

I've been here before and nothing I can do,
I expected it from some, but never from you,
It's beyond my control and deep within my id,
Well, I've tried my best it's all I ever did.

You're Not an Anchor

Hate it when you're worried,
Thinking your actions will drag me down,
Feeling like you're going to be an anchor,
Chained around me so I will drown.

You could not be more wrong,
I'm going to explain it to you,
How your actions make me feel,
You raise me up it's true.

I said I'd be there for you,
I'd support this downward phase,
Those words are meant and real,
I'll hold you through your dark days.

You could never bring me down,
It doesn't matter how much you try,
Just to hold you in my warm embrace,
My spirit soars upwards to the sky.

So don't be scared my wonderful,
You're safe to put your trust in me,
I'll always walk on this journey with you,
On this path that will set you free.

I said I'd be there for you,
I'd support this downward phase,
Those words are meant and real,
I'll hold you through your dark days.

Her Words, My Music, Our Song

Happy in the moment,
Silence in the peace,
Lying in relaxation,
No fearing of alarms.

Warm in the embrace,
Loving envelope enfolded,
Safe within my inner-self,
Relaxed body surround.

Arms reaching for me,
I'm ready to hold and be held,
Not feeling any hesitation,
My feelings more resolved.

So inside and outside,
Locked in two as one,
Finding that inner vibration,
Her words, my music, our song.

Inner Chimp and Anxiety versus Relationships

Well, that caught me off guard,
Stuck in between fight or flight,
The woman in my mind, offering all that I need,
Caught between what choice was right.

Stupid inner chimp, taking over and shutting me down,
Of course, I wanted her more than ever,
But I also needed holding tight,
I was swallowed in her embrace, and it felt so right.

My god I couldn't even kiss her,
I hope she understands this,
The more I wanted her,
Inner Chimp punched me with his fist.

Lying there after she'd gone,
Fuck I wanted to scream to the sky,
Why the hell was I so overwhelmed,
It made me want to crumble and die.

Then I'm on a rampage,
Inner chimp swinging through my mind,
Making me type stupid things,
The sane part of my id, blind.

Telling me I've blown this,
There's no coming back,
I need that chimp back in his cage,
Get him off my back.

Inner chimp and anxiety,
What a total real bad mix,
I've got go sort this out,
Before it's too late to fix.

Some of it's the not knowing,
I'm heading into this blind,
I'm hoping time will tell,
And together we'll be fine.

It's the scary bit, Will my feelings by returned,
I understand she can't make that choice yet,
It scares me and holds me back,
Yet still for her I yearn.

She must understand,
I want her each time more and more,
I think I'm protecting myself from hurt,
Just in case she says no and shuts the door.

So, if we get past this stage,
Let's build up and do it slow,
I can prove how much I desire you,
You'll see it inside me and it will grow.

But I guess I'm lucky,
She told me she knew and understood,
So, I really hope she gets this,
Because for her I feel so much.

Hello You

Hello you,
Thought I'd lost you.
I know blinding isn't it,
You can finally see.

All the colours are shining,
All gleaming again.
I know it's amazing,
The whole world has changed.

Yes, it was quick to happen,
But I still knew you were in there.
It's ok to be scared,
I'll never let you go again.

It's fine to not know the future,
It's fine to be not tethered to the past.
It doesn't mean you've stopped caring,
It means you're free to move on.

Looking forward to tomorrow's,
Not dragged down by the yesterdays.
It is a time for new adventures,
New journeys and new paths.

We can set a course for anywhere,
We don't need a destination.
Just take each day as it comes,
Be open to new opportunities.

Now I've found you,
Let's continue to journeys end.
Now I've found me,
I can start to mend.

To Gain

There isn't much to gain,
Pretending it's the same way.

The tears just mingle with rain,
Washed away, till another day.

But don't give up on life yet,
There's still time to question.

If it doesn't work anyway,
You've done the best you can.

There's hope yet in the pain,
Can't you feel the tension.

Don't be scared to ask,
There's so much you can mention.

It all comes from the past,
It's knocking for your attention.

Don't open that door,
It doesn't mean the pain has lessened.

Bookmarks

Scars are just bookmarks along life's highway,
Just little reminders of times that are past,
Some we cannot see, but forever they last.

Some are the mental wounding inflected upon us,
Some are from our peers because we don't fit the norm,
Some are from scrapes and falls just because.

Some we may think we deserve,
Some others we don't,
Nevertheless, they all bare a story,
Injustice, betrayal, love and hope.

Never cover your scars,
Eventually they will heal,
Everything changes,
Everything heals.

After rain there's always sun,
After dark there's always light,
You don't have to hide your emotions away,
You don't have to be alone in your fight.

Take my hand and heart,
Take that leap of faith,
Hold my hand forever,
Together we can complete this race.

We will stand taller than giants,
Face down the hatred crowd,
Never accept the bullying again,
Our voices full of love and proud.

Never cover your scars,
Eventually they will heal,
Everything changes,
Everything heals.

After rain there's always sun,
After dark there's always light,
You don't have to hide your emotions away,
You don't have to be alone in your fight.

Remember,

Scars are just bookmarks along life's highway.

ABOUT THE AUTHOR

Grew up in the care system of the mid-70's to mid-80's, always told I'd never amount to much, labeled that bad kid, the one your family talks about in whispers. Thought I was just a bad kid, kicking off at school, not interested in having topics forced on me. Much more fun to learn what I wanted too. Eventually left care after countless beatings and lots of different schools, totally uneducated by society standards. Drifting from job to job, relationship to relationship with no real sense of who I really was. But I've always been a voracious reader and loved writing little ditties and poems and poetry. Always kept it mainly to myself as it was my escape avenue. Anyway I'm now a lot older and wiser and realise the issues were down to un-diagnosed autism, not an excuse just a fact. So now I'm surer of myself and just writing. I hope you liked what I put together in this.

Printed in Great Britain
by Amazon